Dear Colin, Ryan
I hope you enjoy the book!
    Love
        Rebecca & Gatsby

Gaby the firedog

Gaby and the Big Red Firedog

A Children's Story

Rebecca Houghton

Fulton Books, Inc.
Meadville, PA

Published by Fulton Books 2021

ISBN 978-1-64654-719-7 (paperback)
ISBN 978-1-64654-714-2 (hardcover)
ISBN 978-1-64654-720-3 (digital)

Printed in the United States of America

I would like to dedicate this book to
all the two-legged and four-legged children in my life.

Gaby was born on a farm. When she was a puppy, she played with horses and birds and her puppy brothers and sisters.

2

When she grew up, she went to live in a big city called Seattle with her human papa and daddy.

Seattle was very different than the farm.

Instead of living in a barn, Gaby lived in a glass tower. Her home was high in the sky. Gaby liked to sit by the window and watch the tiny dogs below.

3

4

Instead of playing in the grass and hearing the birds tweeting, Gaby played on sidewalks and heard cars honking.

But she knew there were other animals in the city, and the loudest was the Big Red Firedog.

"Hoooowl, hooowl, hoo hoo, hooowl," the Big Red Firedog cried through the streets.

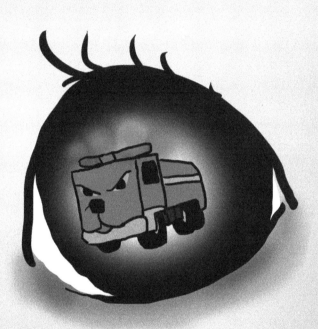

Every time the Big Red Firedog went by, Gaby would run to the window and howl back.

She wanted to meet the Big Red Firedog and have her teach her all about the city.

One day, Papa and Gaby were taking a walk just as the Big Red Firedog went by. *This is my chance!* Gaby thought.

She ran, pulling Papa along.

"Gaby, stop!" Papa called.

But Gaby couldn't stop when she was sure the Big Red Firedog was just around the corner.

Gaby chased her down the street. She ran and ran following the sound, but the city was so noisy it was hard to know where the howling came from.

Gaby turned left, and Gaby turned right, but she couldn't find the Big Red Firedog, and soon she couldn't hear her anymore.

Gaby sat down on the sidewalk, looking around at the tall buildings and realized Papa was gone, and she was lost!

"Oh no! What have I done? Daddy and Papa will be worried about me. How will I ever find my way home?"

9

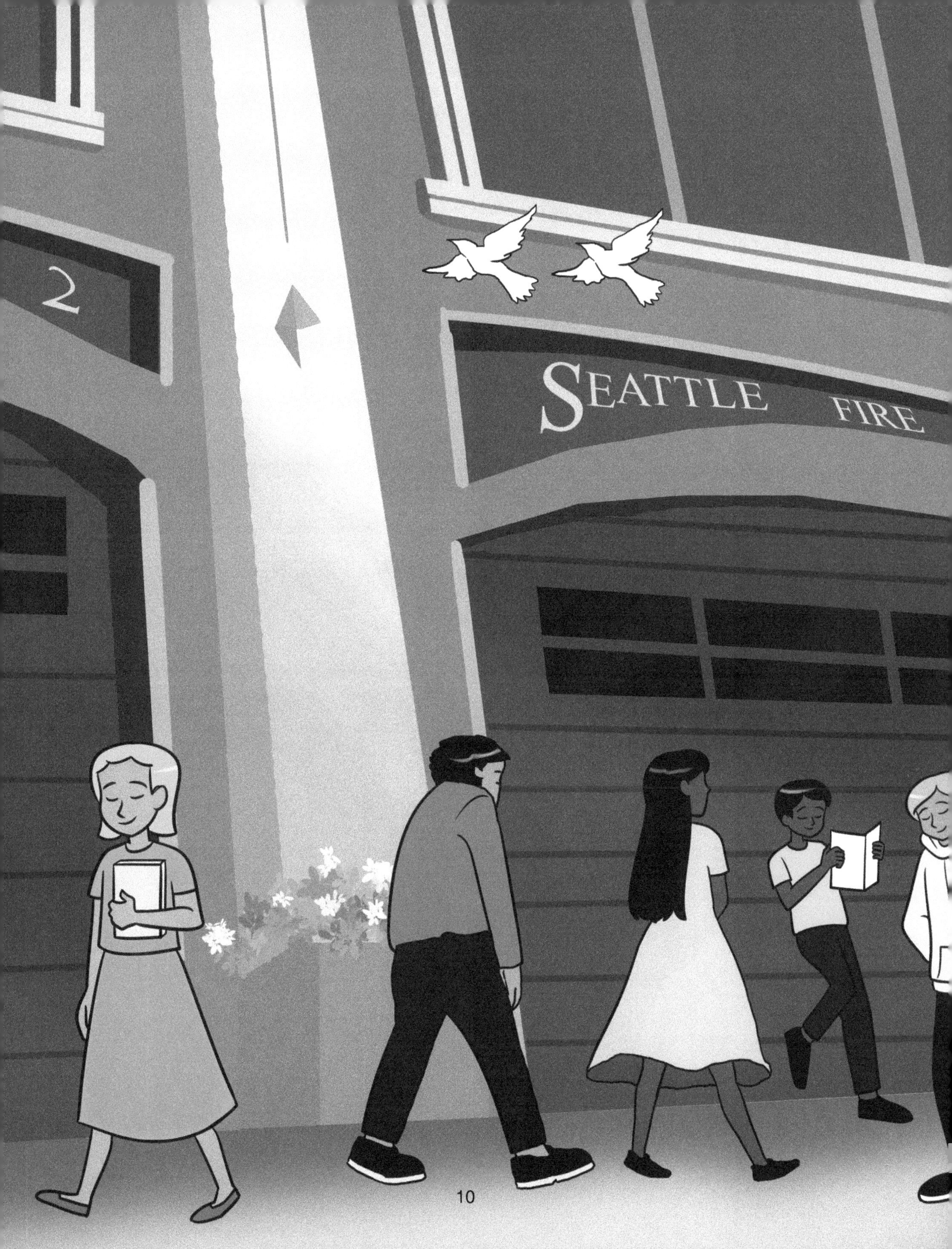
2
SEATTLE FIRE

Just then, the doors of the red brick building that Gaby was sitting in front of opened, and out came a "hooooowl."

It was the Big Red Firedog!

She didn't look much like a dog, but it was definitely the same howl. She swung out of the building and went howling down the street.

If anyone can help me get home, it will be the Big Red Firedog, thought Gaby, chasing after her.

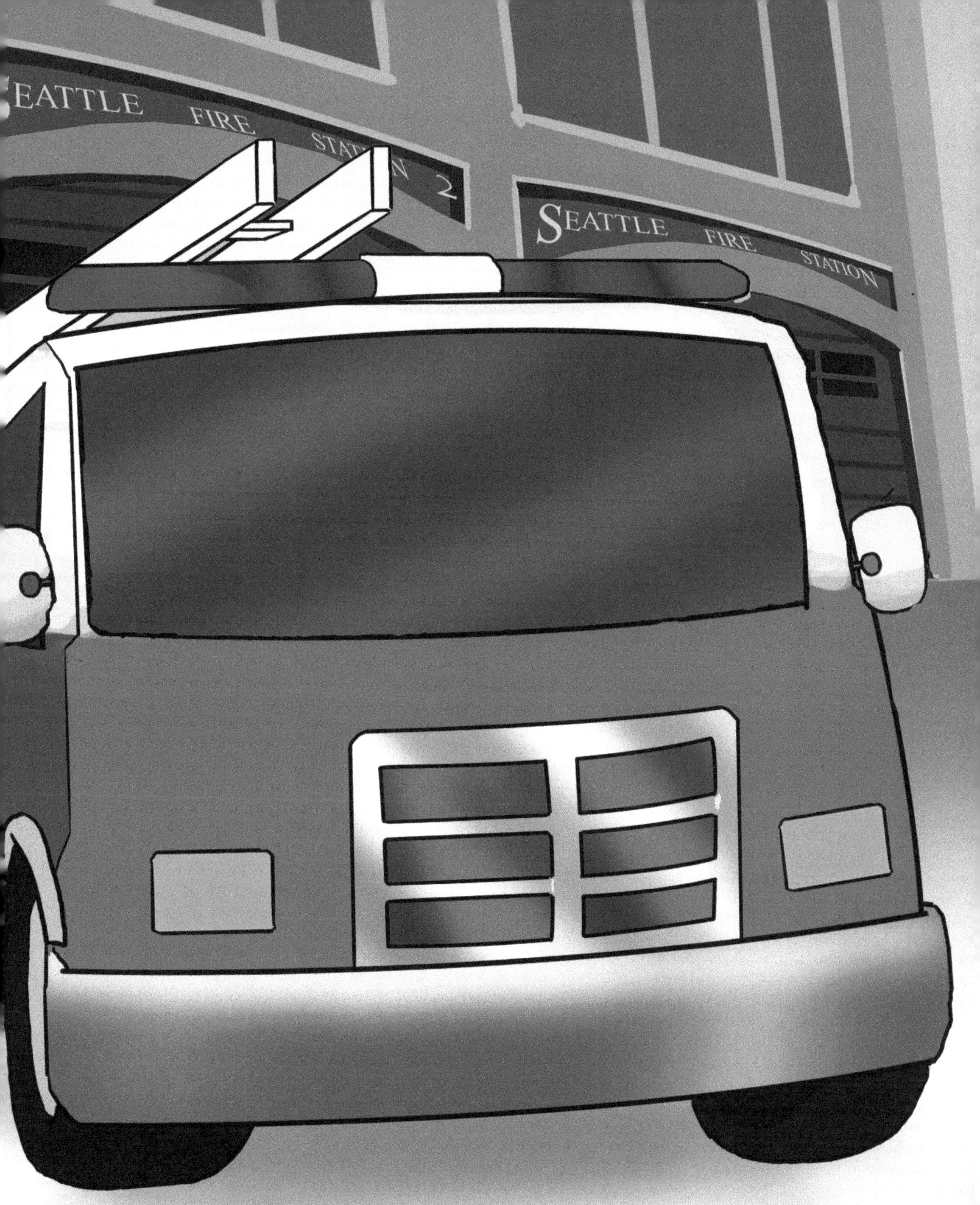
SEATTLE FIRE STATION 2
SEATTLE FIRE STATION

Gaby kept the firedog in her sight until she finally stopped outside a house that was on fire!

Then something strange happened. People started climbing out of the Big Red Firedog and pulling hoses and ladders off her.

Then one of the people who got out of the Big Red Firedog came running out of the house holding a little boy.

"My kitty, my kitty," the little boy cried out.

Gaby heard a different sound. It was a "yeeeooooowl." She looked up and saw a white kitty in the upstairs window.

14

"It's not safe for any people to go back in," said a woman who had got out of the Big Red Firedog.

But Gaby knew she was faster and lighter than people. She could reach the kitty!

She ran past the woman and in through the door.

Smoke filled the room, but the air was clearer near the floor.

Gaby sniffed her way to the kitty, who was still meowing at the window.

"Don't be afraid," Gaby said before she picked the kitty up gently in her mouth and ran back outside.

The little boy and the crowd of people cheered.
"Thank you for saving my kitty," said the boy.
"Are you lost?" said the woman from the Big Red Firedog as she kneeled to read the silver tag on Gaby's collar.
"Yes," Gaby barked. She was suddenly tired and sad again.
"Don't worry, Gaby. We'll get you home."

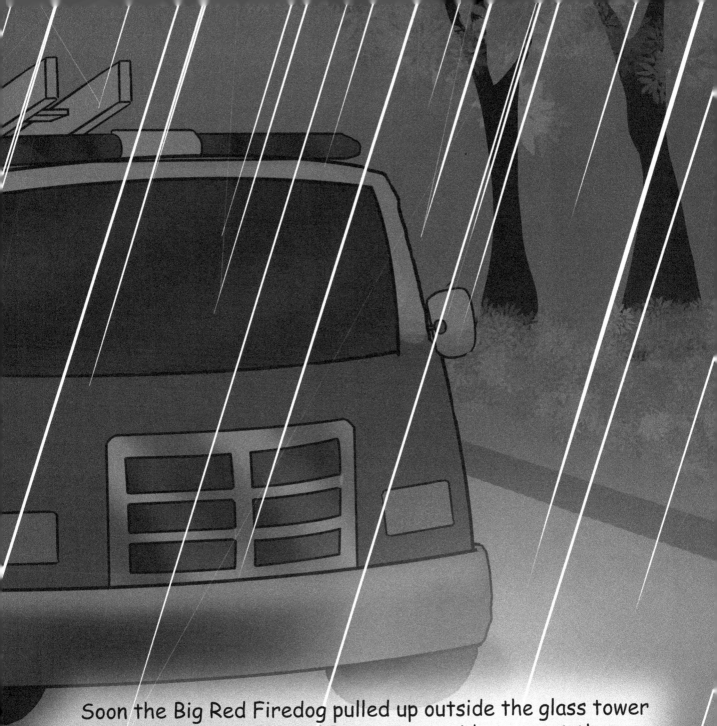

Soon the Big Red Firedog pulled up outside the glass tower with Gaby inside. Daddy and Papa ran outside to meet them.

"Gaby, where have you been?" they cried out with tears running down their cheeks.

Gaby barked, promising to never run off again. She licked her daddy and papa's faces over and over. That night, they all slept together in the big bed.

A few days later, Gaby was taking a walk with Daddy and Papa when she heard the Big Red Firedog howling down the street nearby. Gaby didn't chase after her, but she stopped right by Gaby, and her door opened!

"I thought you'd all like to take a ride around the city," said the firewoman.

Gaby barked to check with Daddy and Papa that it was okay then jumped up into the front passenger seat.

As the Big Red Firedog took off down the street, Gaby put her head out of the window and howled.

About the Author

Rebecca Houghton is a dog mom who also happens to be a writer. Born in England, she emigrated to the United States in 2003 and now lives in Seattle with her spouse and their golden retriever, Gaby, who is a huge fan of their local fire station 2. At Gaby's request, half of all author profits from the sale of this book will be donated equally to the International Association of Firefighters and the Humane Society of the United States. The other half will be spent on dog treats!

Watch Gaby howling with the fire trucks and doing other fun stuff on Instagram @gabythefiredog.

www.rebeccahoughtonwrites.com

CPSIA information can be obtained
at www.ICGtesting.com
Printed in the USA
LVHW070840010721
691077LV00006B/12